Managing Directors: Wang Youbu, Xu Naiqing
Editorial Director: Wu Ying
Editors: Yang Xiaohe, Ginley Regencia

Story and Illustrations: Li Jian
Translation: Yijin Wert

ISBN: 978-1-60220-981-7

Address any comments about *The Little Monkey King's Journey* to:

Better Link Press
99 Park Ave
New York, NY 10016
USA
or
Shanghai Press and Publishing Development Company
F 7 Donghu Road, Shanghai, China (200031)
Email: comments_betterlinkpress@hotmail.com

Printed in China by Shenzhen Donnelley Printing Co., Ltd.

1 3 5 7 9 10 8 6 4 2

The Little Monkey King's Journey

小悟空

Retold in English and Chinese

By Li Jian

Better Link Press

Along the Yellow Sea in China stands the Mountain of Flowers and Fruits.

在中国的黄海边，有一座花果山。

At the foot of the mountain, lay a huge rock. One day a big wave hit the rock and cracked it open with a loud "boom!" A little monkey came out of the broken rock.

在山脚下，有一块巨石。一天，一个大海浪拍打过来，巨石"砰"地一声爆裂开来，从里边跳出来一只小猴。

Although Little Monkey was an orphan, he was very lucky. The Old Monkey King adopted him and treated him as his own child.

尽管小猴无父无母，但他很幸运。老猴王收留了他，待他就像自己的孩子一样。

One day, while playing in the trees, Little Monkey's hands suddenly slipped and he started to fall. The Old Monkey King leaped to catch him. Little Monkey landed safely, but the Old Monkey King was knocked down unconscious.

一天，小猴在树上玩耍，突然手一滑，掉下树来。老猴王纵身一跃，接住了他。小猴安然无恙，老猴王却摔在地上昏迷不醒。

Little Monkey called for the monkey doctor.

The monkey doctor said in despair, "Only the Immortal One can give you a pill that will save the life of the Old Monkey King. He lives on the other side of the ocean, thousands of miles away. No one has ever been there."

小猴赶紧找来猴医。

猴医摇摇头说："猴王的病只有老神仙的药才能治好。他住在大洋另一边，距离这里十万八千里，从来没有人去过那里。"

Little Monkey said with determination, "I will do it! I will find the Immortal One no matter where he is." Little Monkey built himself a bamboo raft, then set out on the voyage.

小猴坚定地说:"我可以,不管天涯海角,我一定能找到老神仙!"他扎了个竹筏,划着它上了路。

The evil Ocean Wind blew the waves as high as a mountain. The Immortal Turtle saw Little Monkey curling into a ball on his raft and asked, "Little Monkey, where are you going? Aren't you afraid of the huge waves?"

"I have to find the Immortal One on the other side of the ocean to get the immortal pill. The Old Monkey King is very badly hurt and I could not stand to see him lying in bed so helpless," Little Monkey said.

顽皮的海风把浪头吹得像山一样高。神龟见小猴缩成一团，就问："小猴，你去哪？这么大的巨浪难道你不怕？"

"我要去找海那边的老神仙求仙药。老猴王受了重伤，我不能眼睁睁看他就这样躺在病床上！"小猴说。

"Don't worry, Little Monkey," said the Immortal Turtle, "I will teach you how to make your body powerful and sturdy so that it can withstand fire, weapons and flood. You will be immortal."

"小猴你别急！"神龟说，"我来教你'金刚不坏身'。有了这个本领，你就不怕火烧、不怕刀斧、不怕水淹，就可以长生不老。"

Little Monkey could only row the bamboo raft a short distance every day and was not getting very far across the sea.

The Phoenixes saw Little Monkey and asked, "Little Monkey, where are you going? Aren't you afraid of the big ocean?"

"I have to find the Immortal One on the other side of the ocean to get the immortal pill. The Old Monkey King is very badly hurt and I could not stand to see him lying in bed so helpless," Little Monkey said.

小猴划着竹筏，一天走不了多少路。

凤和凰看到了小猴："小猴，你去哪？茫茫大海难道你不怕？"

"我要去找海那边的老神仙求仙药，老猴王受了重伤，我不能眼睁睁看他就这样躺在病床上！"小猴说。

"Don't worry, Little Monkey. We will teach you the Seventy-two Transformations. These skills will let you change yourself into any living thing. You can become as small as an ant or as large as a lion. You can transform into a fish and cross the sea much faster than rowing this raft," said the Phoenixes.

"小猴你别急！我们来教你'七十二变'。小到蚂蚁、大到狮子，你想变什么就变什么。你可以变作一条鱼游过大海，可比划竹筏快多了。"凤和凰说。

Little Monkey easily mastered the Seventy-two Transformations, and turned himself into the fastest fish. It only took him half a day to swim across the ocean.

小猴一下子就学会了"七十二变"。他变作一条游得最快的鱼，只用半天时间就游过了大海。

Along the shore a sky-high mountain rose above the water. It was difficult for Little Monkey to climb to the top.

The Dragon King saw Little Monkey and asked, "Little Monkey, where are you going?"

"I have to find the Immortal One on the top of the mountain to get the immortal pill. The Old Monkey King is very badly hurt and I could not stand to see him lying in bed so helpless," Little Monkey said.

海岸边有一座高耸入云的高山，小猴吃力地往上爬。

龙王看见了小猴："小猴，你去哪？"

"我要上山找老神仙求仙药，老猴王受了重伤，我不能眼睁睁看他就这样躺在病床上！"小猴说。

"Don't worry Little Monkey! I will give you a Golden Staff, it is magical and will do as you ask. It can shrink as small as a sewing needle or expand as tall as a pillar to the sky. It will bring you to the top of the mountain," said the Dragon King.

"小猴你别急！我送你一根金箍棒，它很神奇，你想什么它就能变成什么。它可以缩成像绣花针那么小，也可以变成像擎天柱那么高，把你送到山顶上！"龙王说。

Little Monkey held on tightly to the Golden Staff and called on it to grow taller and taller. In the blink of an eye, he reached the top of the mountain.

小猴抱紧金箍棒，嘴里念着："变长！变长！"一眨眼就到了山顶上。

Little Monkey spotted the temple at the top of the mountain where the Immortal One lived.

小猴找到了山顶上那座老神仙居住的道观。

Little Monkey went inside and immediately fell to his knees with a big "thud" in front of the Immortal One.

"Merciful Immortal, my Old Monkey King is very badly hurt. I beg you to cure him!"

"Don't worry, Little Monkey. I know everything about you. I will give you the new name of Sun Wukong. I will teach you all the skills of an Immortal, and then you will be able to save your king's life."

小猴进去了以后，"扑通"一声跪在老神仙面前。

"慈悲的老神仙！老猴王受了重伤，求您快帮忙治好他！"

"小猴你别急！你的事我全知道。我送你一个名字'孙悟空'，教会你仙术和本领，你就能把猴王救醒。"

The Immortal One taught Little Wukong how to do a cloud somersault, which covers 108,000 *li* (or 33,554 miles) in a single flip.

老神仙教会了小悟空"筋斗云",一个跟头能跑出十万八千里。

One day, the Immortal One put a pill in Little Wukong's hand and said, "You have learned all the necessary skills. Take this red immortal pill and return to the Mountain of Flowers and Fruits to save your king."

有一天，老神仙将一枚仙丹放在小悟空的手里说："你已学成，快回花果山吧，这颗红色的仙丹能帮你救醒老猴王。"

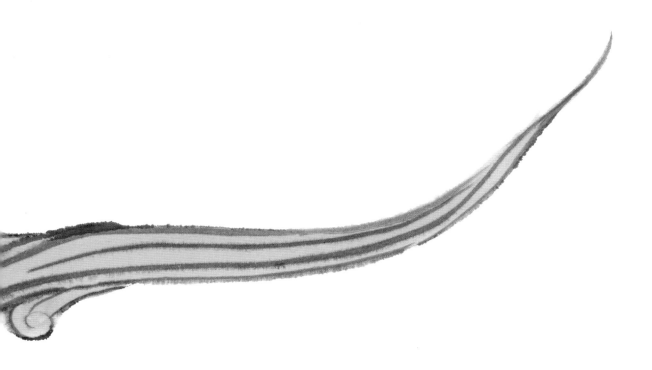

Little Wukong used his cloud-traveling power and returned to the Mountain of Flowers and Fruits in a single cloud somersault.

小悟空腾云又驾雾，一个跟头就回到了花果山。

Little Wukong put the immortal pill into the mouth of the Old Monkey King. The Old Monkey King let out a long breath and gradually opened his eyes. Little Wukong was so excited that he embraced the Old Monkey King tightly with tears and laughter.

小悟空把仙丹放进了老猴王的嘴里。老猴王吐出一口污气，睁开了眼睛。小悟空高兴极了，抱着他又哭又笑。

Little Wukong not only saved the life of the Old Monkey King, he also used the power and skills he gained to help others. Everybody came to him whenever they had trouble. From then on, the Mountain of Flowers and Fruits was filled with laughter and happiness.

Later on when he was grown, Little Wukong became the Monkey King.

小悟空不仅救了老猴王，还用自己的一身本领帮助他人，谁有困难都会找悟空帮忙。从此，花果山上到处是幸福和欢笑。

小悟空长大后成为了美猴王。